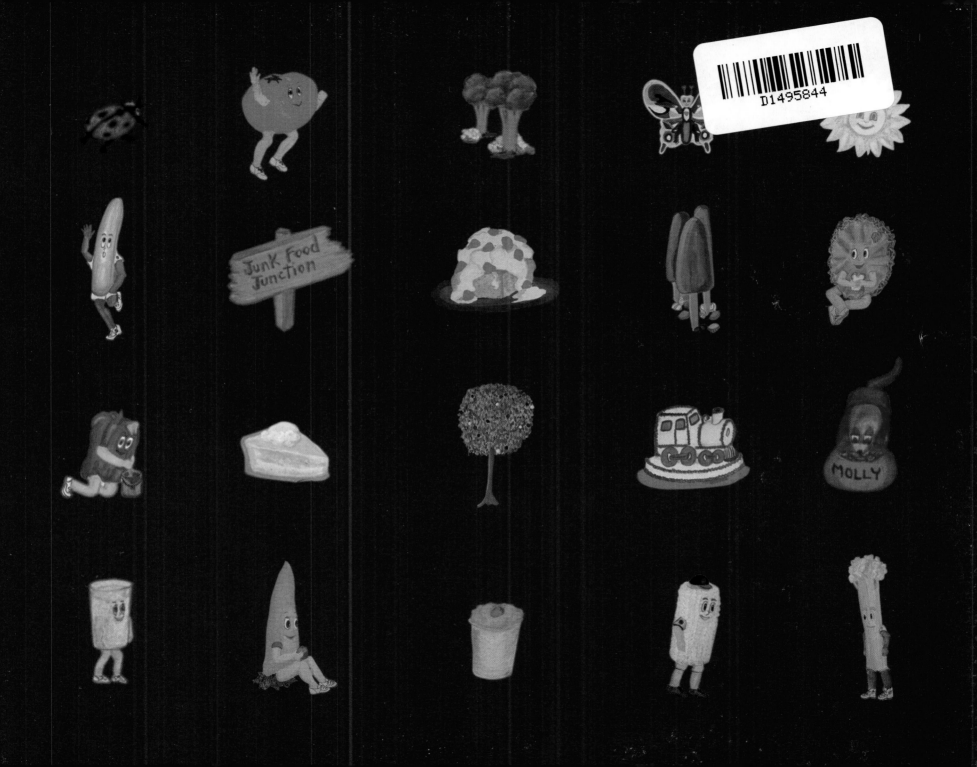

Freddy & Flossy Flutterby

Written & illustrated by Ann Douglas

This book honors Deanna Galante and her unborn child. She worked at the WTC as a securities officer and my son worked there as a bond broker. Fred and Deanna were together on 9-11, the last day of their lives. How we live our lives will honor our loved ones the most. They will live in our hearts forever.

Love, faith and hope, Ann

Acknowledgements

I am fortunate to have my beloved husband Mike, who encouraged me from the very start to preserve a wonderful set of childhood memories from a time when the world was truly a better place. "Keep your vision, and everything else will follow," he urged me.

A Mother's love to Nancy and her fiancé Rob and to Susanne and her husband Rick for their love and devotion during the metamorphosis of this project. Rob's painted logo, Nancy's technical skills, Susanne's presentation to her kindergartners and Rick's editing finesse all contributed to making this dream come true. A Grandmother's love to Timmy, whose smiles have lighted the way when the path was sad and dark.

I am very thankful for Rosemary Daniell and Zona Rosa, the series of writing groups she started in Savannah and now leads all over the world, where I realized that I could write and paint my dreams. My deep gratitude goes to cousin Nancy Cardwell, professional editor and writer, for giving the story of *Freddy & Flossy Flutterby* continuity. Also, much appreciation goes to Laurie Shock for her Spartan efforts and a brilliant book design.

Thank you, Martha, my twin—you have supported me through hard times; and Kris, my Lake-sister, for telling me the truth when I wouldn't listen to anyone else. Dearest Jules, thank you for your wonderful words of encouragement and for teaching us, "It doesn't matter what you do in art…as long as it isn't you doing it." Your "Communing with the Power" saved my life. And my friend from childhood, Bailey White, your suggestions were great gifts. Mama's namesake, you are family.

A Mother's undying love to my late son Fred, who adored this book, and always believed in it and in the message of love and forgiveness. This is for you, my Darling! You will always be with us. As you always said, we shall do what we love, and love what we do. I believe with all my heart that those words can and will make this world a better place.

Published by Betta Place, Inc.
436 Ivy Street
Jesup, GA 31546

Copyright ©2002 Betta Place, Inc.
Printed in Canada

LC# 2002110177

ISBN# 0-9723184-0-2

5 4 3 2 1   02 03 04 05 06

First Edition

Edited by John Yow & Associates

Book design and production by Shock Design, Inc.
shockdesign@mindspring.com

Jacket design by Shock Design, Inc. and Rob Nason

Freddy & Flossy Flutterby title typography by Rob Nason

SUE

FREDDY

NAN

Flossy

One bright sunny morning, Sue and Nan and their brother Freddy were playing down by the creek. They were looking at the fish and the bugs and the birds when a beautiful butterfly fluttered into view.

"Hi," she said, "I'm Flossy Flutterby."

Flossy flew over toward Freddy and hovered lightly in the air above him. "Freddy," she said, "do you remember when Jamie and Tommy wanted to chop up that big caterpillar you found in the woods, and you said no? Remember how you took it to school for 'Show and Tell,' then turned it loose in the woods during recess?"

"Ummmm, hmmmm," nodded Freddy.

"Well, I was that caterpillar," exclaimed Flossy. "I turned into a butterfly! Freddy, you saved my life!"

Freddie grinned. His blue-green eyes grew round like crystal marbles.

2

Flossy turned to Sue and Nan and asked, "Would you all like to go on a trip with me? Run ask your mother. Tell her we'll be home before supper." Sue ran to the house to ask and returned with their mother's permission.

The children suddenly found themselves lifted into the air on a puffy, fluffy white cloud, while Flossy directed the way.

"We're going to Betta Place," she announced. "It's called that because it truly is a better place. Everyone there is treated equally, and love and kindness rule the hearts of everyone who lives there."

When the cloud landed, Sue and Nan and Freddy were astonished to see giant broccoli trees, lima bean rocks, and cauliflower bushes. They were even more astonished at the people who greeted them—they appeared to be walking, talking fruits and vegetables.

"The Fruit and Vegetable People aren't really plants," explained Flossy. "They're people who have given their lives to growing fruit and vegetables and sending them to hungry children around the world. Each one represents the plant he or she has worked so hard for, but they have real hearts and minds and feelings, just like other people."

"It's magic." Flossy swooped and spun happily. "When your heart is filled with love, anything is possible. That's why I can talk."

6

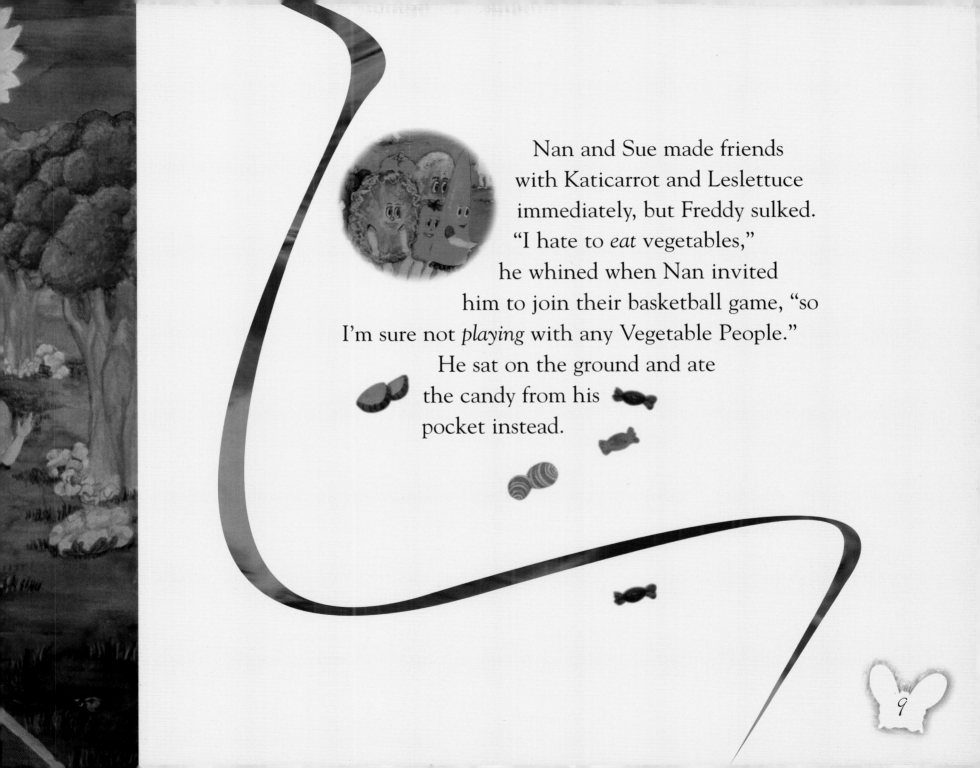

Nan and Sue made friends
with Katicarrot and Leslettuce
immediately, but Freddy sulked.
"I hate to *eat* vegetables,"
he whined when Nan invited
him to join their basketball game, "so
I'm sure not *playing* with any Vegetable People."
He sat on the ground and ate
the candy from his
pocket instead.

After playing basketball, Sue, Nan, Katicarrot, and Leslettuce planned a picnic. They went inside Betta Place Building to shop for the things they would need, but Freddy stayed outside to watch a couple of the Vegetable People paint a mural on the building's side. He noticed that Flossy was included in the picture and asked why.

The Vegetable People explained that Flossy appears to children around the world and brings them love. "So we put her in every picture we paint," they added with pride.

Freddy remembered how the glitter on Flossy's wings sparkled in the light. He believed what they said about Flossy. "Flossy is like a diamond in the sun," he thought.

On a grassy hill next to Milky Way Lane, Sue, Nan, Katicarrot, and Leslettuce spread out a beautiful blue blanket and unloaded a basket full of food. It was from all the best places in Betta Place: Veg Avenue, Fruity-Loop, Milky Way Lane, Meat Street, Grain Lane, and Treat Street.

While the girls set about enjoying their their feast, Freddy wandered away. He wasn't hungry at all. He had been munching candy all morning.

At the bottom of the hill, Freddy met a boy wearing a tee-shirt with "JJ" printed on it.

"It stands for Junk Food Junky," the boy explained. "Come on with me," he urged Freddy, "and let me show you Junk Food Junction, where I live. It's a place where we don't do homework, we don't do chores, we don't brush our teeth. We stay up late. And . . . we never eat vegetables!"

That sounded like a fantastic place to Freddy, so he and the "JJ" hopped aboard the Junk Food Junction Express. He didn't even tell his sisters.

But Freddy hadn't been in Junk Food Junction very long before he discovered that it wasn't such a wonderful place after all. The Junk Food Junkies circled around to tease and frighten him. The children were mean, and they solved problems by fighting. They taunted other children who were different and called them names. They laughed when anyone fell down.

It was also a dirty place, with litter everywhere, and bugs in the food, and a stale smell in the air that stuck in your nose.

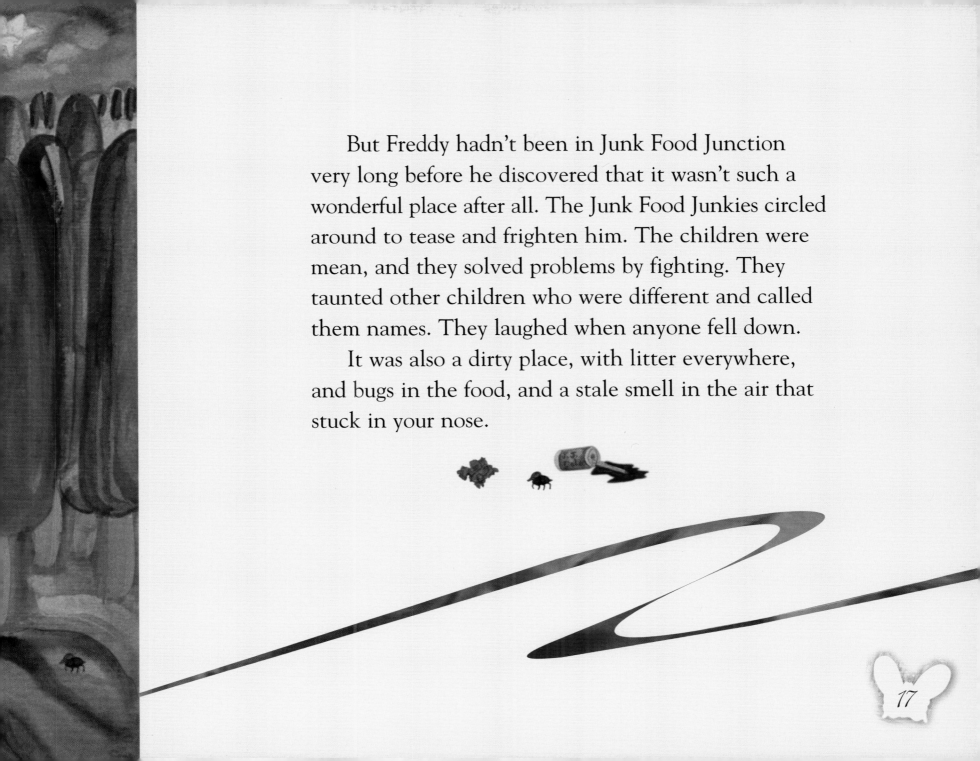

17

Miserable and lonely, Freddy knew that he had made a mistake.

"I have to get back to Betta Place for a picnic with my sisters," he said, blinking back his tears. "They don't even know where I am!"

But the Junk Food Junkies hooted! "Go back where you came from?" one of them shouted. "You never will!"

"Yesterday," said another, "a kid named Derrick ran away, and when we find him . . . POW! But right now, I dare you to ride Derrick's bike down Bugaboo Hill."

18

Back at Betta Place, Katicarrot, Sue, Leslettuce, and Nan were looking everywhere for Freddy. He wasn't on Veg Avenue, Fruity-Loop, Milky Way Lane, Meat Street, or Grain Lane. Their hearts were broken. Without their brother Freddy, nothing would be the same!

Then they remembered Treat Street.
Surely Freddy would be there, trying to find
something sweet to eat. But no one on
Treat Street had seen Freddy. Sue and
Nan began to cry. Freddy was lost.
How could they ever go home without
their precious brother?

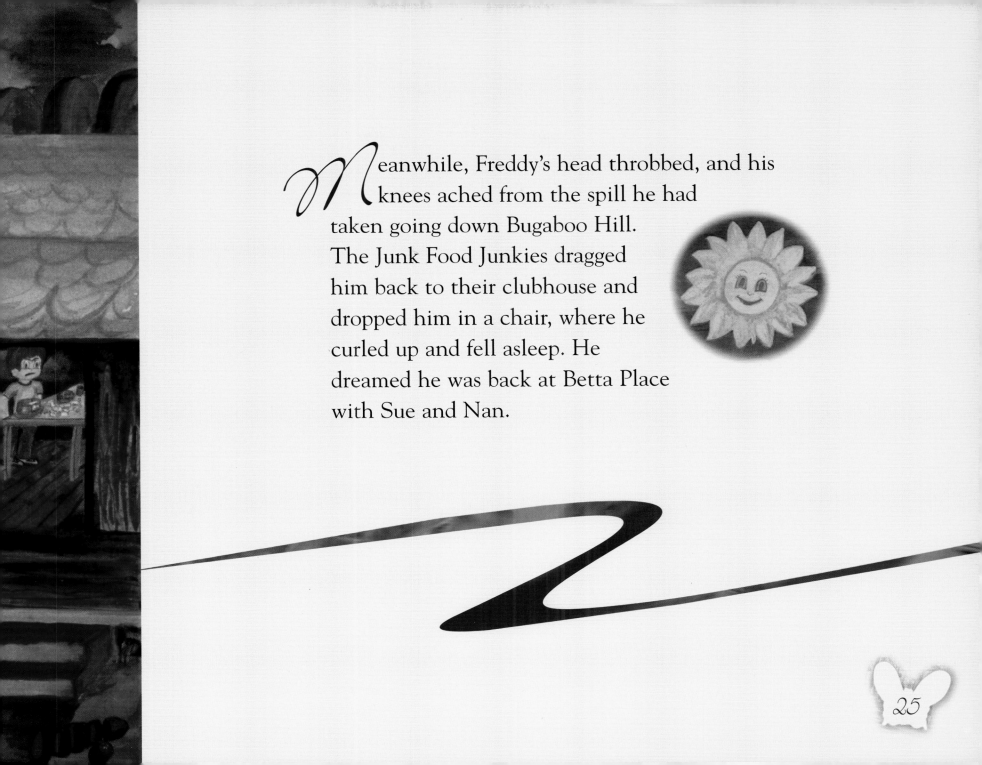

Meanwhile, Freddy's head throbbed, and his knees ached from the spill he had taken going down Bugaboo Hill. The Junk Food Junkies dragged him back to their clubhouse and dropped him in a chair, where he curled up and fell asleep. He dreamed he was back at Betta Place with Sue and Nan.

When he woke up, Freddy saw that no one was
watching him, so he crept around behind the clubhouse, then ran down toward the train tracks. On his
way through the deep dark Junk Food Junction Forest,
he came upon Derrick, alone and crying.

"Oh, Freddy, you're here too? Isn't it terrible?" he
wailed. "I miss my mama, my clean white shirts, and
my favorite friends. And I *hate* it down here!"

"It is horrible here," echoed Freddy.

26

Suddenly Flossy appeared before their tear-filled eyes. Both Freddy and Derrick hung their heads in shame.

"Flossy," said Freddy, "we're so sorry we ran away. We miss our mama and daddy, but the kids here say we can't go home."

Flossy smiled. "Of course you can go home. And when you get there, your parents will give you a big hug. Because *forgiveness is free!* It doesn't cost a dime and you can have it anytime. As long as you ask from your heart."

Just then the train appeared—the Betta Place Special—and slowed to a stop. The two boys jumped on, and *clickety-clack, clickety-clack*, they went back. They had escaped the Junk Food Junky attack.

Freddy and Derrick stepped off the train and into the warm sunshine of Betta Place. Freddy thought he could hear the wind whispering his favorite song. 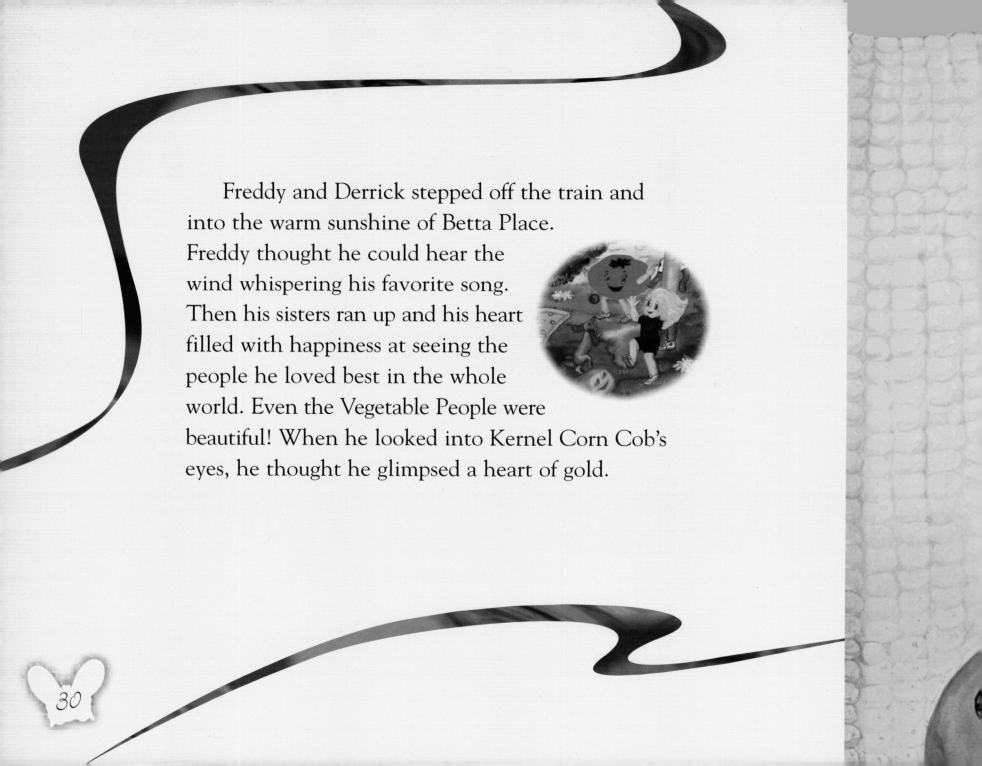 Then his sisters ran up and his heart filled with happiness at seeing the people he loved best in the whole world. Even the Vegetable People were beautiful! When he looked into Kernel Corn Cob's eyes, he thought he glimpsed a heart of gold.

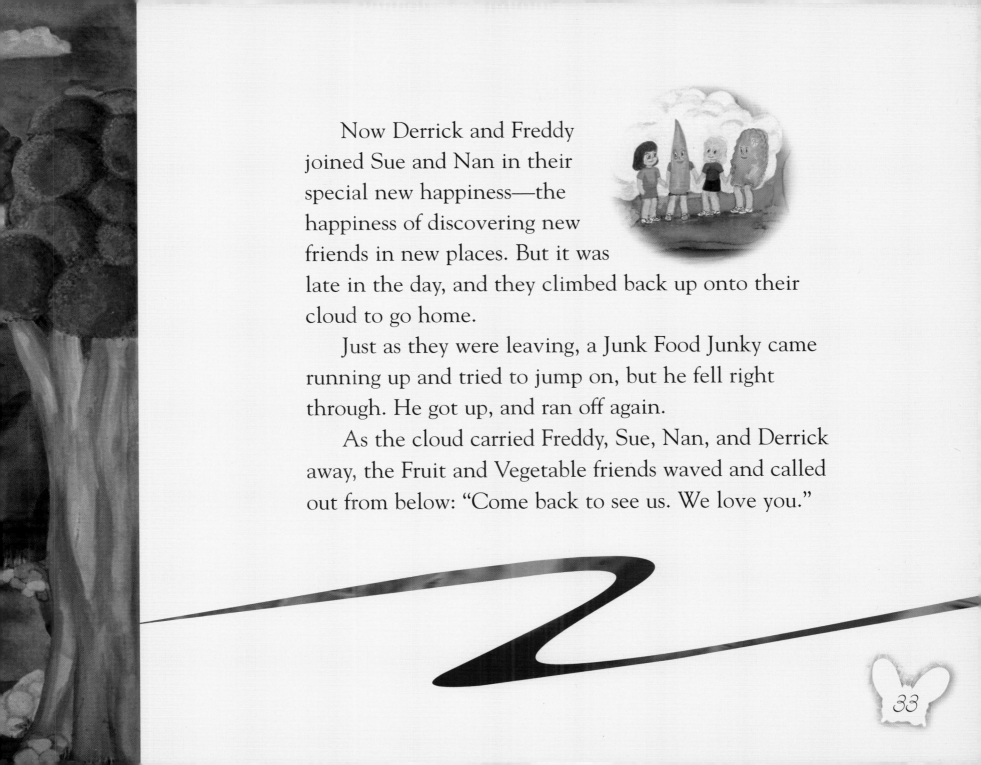

Now Derrick and Freddy joined Sue and Nan in their special new happiness—the happiness of discovering new friends in new places. But it was late in the day, and they climbed back up onto their cloud to go home.

Just as they were leaving, a Junk Food Junky came running up and tried to jump on, but he fell right through. He got up, and ran off again.

As the cloud carried Freddy, Sue, Nan, and Derrick away, the Fruit and Vegetable friends waved and called out from below: "Come back to see us. We love you."

Back home that night at supper, Dad was surprised. "Freddy . . . you're eating your vegetables!"

Freddy squirmed in his chair, remembering how well the Fruit and Vegetable People had treated him and his sisters. "Well," he said, "these green beans aren't so bad."

Dad beamed with pride. "You are all growing up so fast."

Just then Flossy fluttered by the window. Sue, Nan, and Freddy all saw her there, but when Dad turned to see what they were smiling at, all he saw was gold and silver glitter, gently settling to earth.

We love you, Freddy!